# The
# of the Books

by

# Jonathan Swift

ALMA CLASSICS

ALMA CLASSICS

an imprint of ALMA BOOKS LTD
3 Castle Yard
Richmond
Surrey TW10 6TF
United Kingdom
www.almaclassics.com

First published in 1704
First published by Alma Classics in 2012
This new paperback edition first published by Alma Classics in 2016

Printed in Great Britain by CPI Group (UK) Ltd, Croydon CR0 4YY

ISBN: 978-1-84749-679-9

# Contents

# The Battle
# of the Books

# The Bookseller to the Reader

The following discourse, as it is unquestionably of the same author, so it seems to have been written about the same time with the former – I mean when the famous dispute was on foot about ancient and modern learning. The controversy took its rise from an essay of Sir William Temple's upon that subject, which was answered by W. Wotton BD, with an appendix by Dr Bentley, endeavouring to destroy the credit of Aesop and Phalaris for authors whom Sir William Temple had in the essay before mentioned highly commended. In that appendix, the Doctor falls hard upon a new edition of Phalaris put out by the Honourable Charles Boyle (now Earl of Orrery), to which Mr Boyle replied at large with great learning and wit – and the Doctor, voluminously, rejoined.* In this dispute, the town highly resented to see a person of Sir William Temple's character and merits roughly used by the two reverend gentlemen aforesaid, and without any manner of provocation. At length, there appearing no end of the quarrel, our author tells us that the books in St James's library, looking upon themselves as parties principally concerned, took up the controversy and came to a decisive battle. But the manuscript by the injury of fortune or weather being in several places imperfect, we cannot learn to which side the victory fell.

I must warn the Reader to beware of applying to persons what is here meant only of books in the most literal sense. So, when Virgil is mentioned, we are not to understand the person of a famous poet called by that name, but only certain sheets of paper bound up in leather containing in print the works of the said poet – and so of the rest.

# The Preface of the Author

Satire is a sort of glass wherein beholders do generally discover everybody's face but their own – which is the chief reason for that kind of reception it meets in the world, and that so very few are offended with it. But if it should happen otherwise, the danger is not great, and I have learnt from long experience never to apprehend mischief from those understandings I have been able to provoke, for anger and fury, though they add strength to the sinews of the body, yet are found to relax those of the mind, and to render all its efforts feeble and impotent.

There is a brain that will endure but one scumming: let the owner gather it with discretion and manage his little stock with husbandry, but of all things let him beware of bringing it under the lash of his betters, because that will make it all bubble up into impertinence, and he will find no new supply – wit without knowledge being a sort of cream which gathers in a night to the top and by a skilful hand may be soon whipped into froth, but once scummed away, what appears underneath will be fit for nothing but to be thrown to the hogs.

# The Battle of the Books

*A full and true account of the battle fought
last Friday between the ancient and the
modern books in St James's Library.*

Whoever examines with due circumspection
into the annual records of time will find it
remarked that "war is the child of pride" and
"pride the daughter of riches"* – the former
of which assertions may be soon granted.
But one cannot so easily subscribe to the
latter, for pride is nearly related to beggary

and want, either by father or mother, and sometimes by both, and to speak naturally it very seldom happens among men to fall out when all have enough: invasions usually travelling from north to south – that is to say, from poverty to plenty. The most ancient and natural grounds of quarrels are lust and avarice – which, though we may allow to be brethren or collateral branches of pride, are certainly the issues of want. For, to speak in the phrase of writers upon the politics,* we may observe in the republic of dogs (which in its original seems to be an institution of the many) that the whole state is ever in the profoundest peace after a full meal; and that civil broils arise among them when it happens for one great bone to be seized on by some leading dog, who either divides it among the few, and then it falls to an oligarchy, or keeps it to himself, and then it runs up to a tyranny. The same reasoning also holds place among them in those dissensions we behold upon a turgescency in any of their females. For, the right of possession lying in common (it being impossible to establish a property in so delicate a case), jealousies and suspicions do so abound that the whole commonwealth of that street is reduced to a manifest state of war of every citizen against every citizen, till someone of more courage, conduct or fortune than the rest seizes and enjoys the prize – upon which naturally arises plenty of heartburning and envy and snarling against the happy dog. Again, if we look upon any of these republics engaged in a foreign war, either of invasion or defence, we shall find the same reasoning will serve as to the grounds and occasions of each, and that poverty or want, in some degree or other (whether real or in opinion, which makes no alteration in the case) has a great share, as well as pride, on the part of the aggressor.

Now, whoever will please to take this scheme and either reduce or adapt it to an intellectual state or commonwealth of learning will soon discover the first ground of disagreement between the two great parties at this time in arms, and form just conclusions upon the merits of either cause. But the issue or events of this war are not so easy to conjecture at, for the present quarrel is so inflamed by the warm heads of either faction, and the pretensions somewhere or other so exorbitant, as not to admit the least overtures of accommodation. This quarrel first began (as I have heard it affirmed by an old dweller in the neighbourhood) about a small spot of ground lying and being upon one of the two tops of the hill Parnassus, the highest and largest of which had, it seems, been time out of mind in quiet possession of certain tenants called the Ancients, and the other was held by the Moderns. But these, disliking their present station, sent certain ambassadors to the Ancients complaining of a great nuisance – how the height of that part of Parnassus quite spoilt the prospect of theirs, especially towards the east* – and therefore, to avoid a war, offered them the choice of this alternative: either that the Ancients would please to remove themselves and their effects down to the lower summity,* which the Moderns would graciously surrender to them, and advance in their place, or else that the said Ancients will give leave to the Moderns to come with shovels and mattocks and level the said hill as low as they shall think it convenient. To which the Ancients made answer how little they expected such a message as this, from a colony whom they had admitted out of their own free grace to so near a neighbourhood. That as to their own seat, they were aborigines of it, and therefore, to talk with them of a removal or surrender, was a language they did not understand. That if the height of the hill, on their side, shortened the prospect of the Moderns, it was a disadvantage they could not help, but desired them to consider whether that injury (if it be any) were not largely recompensed by the shade and shelter it afforded them. That as to levelling or digging down, it was either folly or ignorance to propose it, if they did or did not know how that side of the hill was an entire rock, which would break their tools and hearts, without any damage to itself. That they would therefore advise the Moderns rather to raise their own side of the hill than dream of pulling down that of the Ancients – to the former of which they would not only give licence, but also largely contribute. All this was rejected by the Moderns with much indignation, who still insisted upon one of the two expedients. And so this difference broke out into a long and obstinate war,* maintained on the one part by resolution and by the courage of certain leaders and allies, but on the other by the greatness of their number, upon all defeats, affording continual recruits. In this quarrel, whole rivulets of ink have been exhausted, and the virulence of both parties enormously augmented. Now it must here be understood that ink is the great missive weapon in all battles of the learned – which, conveyed through a sort of engine called a quill, infinite numbers of these are darted at the enemy by the valiant on each side with equal skill and violence, as if it were an engagement of porcupines. This malignant liquor was compounded by the engineer who invented it of two ingredients, which are gall and copperas, by its bitterness and venom to suit in some degree, as well as to foment, the genius of the combatants. And as the Grecians after an engagement when they could not agree about the victory were wont to set up trophies on both sides,* the beaten party being content to be at the same expense to keep itself in countenance (a laudable and ancient custom, happily revived of late,* in the art of war), so the learned, after a sharp and bloody dispute, do on both sides hang out their trophies too, whichever comes by the worst. These trophies have largely inscribed on them the merits of the cause, a full impartial account of such a battle and how the victory fell clearly to the party that set them up. They are known to the world under several names: as disputes, arguments, rejoinders, brief considerations, answers, replies, remarks, reflections, objections, confutations. For a very few days they are fixed up in all public places, either by themselves or their representatives* for passengers to gaze at – from whence the chiefest and largest are removed to certain magazines they call libraries, there to remain in a quarter purposely assigned them, and from thenceforth begin to be called books of controversy.

In these books is wonderfully instilled and preserved the spirit of each warrior while he is alive,* and after his death his soul transmigrates there to inform them.* This, at least, is the more common opinion, but I believe it is with libraries as with other cemeteries, where some philosophers affirm that a certain spirit, which they call *brutum hominis*,* hovers over the monument till the body is corrupted and turns to dust or to worms, but then vanishes or dissolves. So, we may say, a restless spirit haunts over every book till dust or worms have seized upon it – which to some may happen in a few days, but to others later, and therefore books of controversy, being of all others haunted by the most disorderly spirits, have always been confined in a separate lodge from the rest, and for fear of mutual violence against each other it was thought prudent by our ancestors to bind them to the peace with strong iron chains.* Of which invention the original occasion was this: when the works of Scotus first came out, they were carried to a certain great library and had lodgings appointed them, but this author was no sooner settled than he went to visit his master Aristotle, and there both concerted together to seize Plato by main force and turn him out from his ancient station among the divines, where he had peaceably dwelt near eight hundred years.* The attempt succeeded, and the two usurpers have reigned ever since in his stead. But to maintain quiet for the future, it was decreed that all polemics of the larger size should be held fast with a chain.

By this expedient, the public peace of libraries might certainly have been preserved if a new species of controversial books had not arose of late years, instinct with a most malignant spirit, from the war above-mentioned between the learned about the higher summity of Parnassus.

When these books were first admitted into the public libraries, I remember to have said upon occasion to several persons concerned how I was sure they would create broils wherever they came unless a world of care were taken. And therefore I advised that the champions of each side should be coupled together or otherwise mixed, that like the blending of contrary poisons their malignity might be employed among themselves. And it seems I was neither an ill prophet nor an ill counsellor, for it was nothing else but the neglect of this caution which gave occasion to the terrible fight that happened on Friday last between the ancient and modern books in the

King's Library. Now, because the talk of this battle is so fresh in everybody's mouth and the expectation of the town so great to be informed in the particulars, I – being possessed of all qualifications requisite in a historian and retained by neither party – have resolved to comply with the urgent importunity of my friends by writing down a full impartial account thereof.

The Guardian of the Regal Library,* a person of great valour, but chiefly renowned for his humanity,* had been a fierce champion for the Moderns, and in an engagement upon Parnassus had vowed with his own hands to knock down two of the Ancient chiefs* who guarded a small pass on the superior rock, but endeavouring to climb up was cruelly obstructed by his own unhappy weight and tendency towards his centre – a quality to which those of the Modern party are extreme subject, for being light-headed they have in speculation a wonderful agility and conceive nothing too high for them to mount, but in reducing to practice discover a mighty pressure about their posteriors and their heels. Having thus failed in his design, the disappointed champion bore a cruel rancour to the Ancients, which he resolved to gratify by showing all marks of his favour to the books of their adversaries and lodging them in the fairest apartments – when at the same time, whatever book had the boldness to own itself for an advocate of the Ancients, was buried alive in some obscure corner and threatened upon the least displeasure to be turned out of doors. Besides, it so happened that about this time there was a strange confusion of place among all the books in the library,* for which several reasons were assigned. Some imputed it to a great heap of learned dust, which a perverse wind blew off from a shelf of Moderns into the keeper's eyes. Others affirmed he had a humour to pick the worms out of the schoolmen and swallow them fresh and fasting, whereof some fell upon his spleen and some climbed up into his head, to the great perturbation of both. And lastly, others maintained that by walking much in the dark about the library he had quite lost the situation of it out of his head, and therefore, in replacing his books, he was apt to mistake and clap

Descartes next to Aristotle. Poor Plato had got between Hobbes and the *Seven Wise Masters*,* and Virgil was hemmed in with Dryden* on one side and Withers* on the other.

Meanwhile, those books that were advocates for the Moderns chose out one from among them to make a progress through the whole library, examine the number and strength of their party and concert their affairs. This messenger performed all things very industriously and brought back with him a list of their forces, in all fifty thousand, consisting chiefly of light-horse, heavy-armed foot and mercenaries – whereof the foot were in general but sorrily armed and worse clad, their horses large but extremely out of case and heart. However, some few by trading among the Ancients had furnished themselves tolerably enough.

While things were in this ferment, discord grew extremely high, hot words passed on both sides, and ill blood was plentifully bred. Here a solitary Ancient, squeezed up among a whole shelf of Moderns, offered fairly to dispute the case and to prove by manifest reasons that the priority was due to them from long possession and in regard of their prudence, antiquity and, above all, their great merits towards the Moderns. But these denied the premises and seemed very much to wonder how the Ancients could pretend to insist upon their antiquity, when it was so plain (if they went to that) the Moderns were much the more ancient of the two.* As for any obligations they owed to the Ancients, they renounced them all.

"'Tis true," said they, "we are informed some few of our party have been so mean to borrow their subsistence from you; but the rest, infinitely the greater number (and especially we French and English), were so far from stooping to so base an example that there never passed, till this very hour, six words between us. For our horses are of our own breeding, our arms of our own forging and our clothes of our own cutting-out and sewing."

Plato was by chance upon the next shelf and, observing those that spoke to be in the ragged plight mentioned a while ago – their jades lean and foundered, their weapons of rotten wood, their armour rusty and nothing but rags underneath – he laughed loud, and in his pleasant way swore, by God, he believed them.

Now, the Moderns had not proceeded in their late negotiation with secrecy enough to escape the notice of the enemy. For those advocates who had begun the quarrel by setting first on foot the dispute of precedency talked so loud of coming to a battle that Temple happened to overhear them and gave immediate intelligence to the Ancients, who thereupon drew up their scattered troops together, resolving to act upon the defensive – upon which, several of the Moderns fled over to their party, and among the rest Temple himself. This Temple, having been educated and long conversed* among the Ancients, was of all the Moderns their greatest favourite, and became their greatest champion.

Things were at this crisis when a material accident fell out. For, upon the highest corner of a large window, there dwelt a certain spider, swollen up to the first magnitude by the destruction of infinite numbers of flies, whose spoils lay scattered before the gates of his palace like human bones before the cave of some giant. The avenues to his castle were guarded with turnpikes and palisades, after all the modern way of fortification.* After you had passed several courts, you came to the centre, wherein you might behold the constable himself in his own lodgings, which had windows fronting to each avenue and ports to sally out upon all occasions of prey or defence. In this mansion he had for some time dwelt in peace and plenty, without danger to his person by swallows from above or to his palace by brooms from below, when it was the pleasure of fortune to conduct thither a wandering bee, to whose curiosity a broken pane in the glass had discovered itself. And in he went, where – expatiating a while – he at last happened to alight upon one of the outward walls of the spider's citadel which, yielding to the unequal weight, sunk down to the very foundation. Thrice he endeavoured to force his passage, and thrice the centre shook. The spider within, feeling the terrible convulsion, supposed at first that Nature was approaching to her final dissolution, or else that Beelzebub,* with all his legions, was come to revenge the death of many thousands of his subjects, whom this enemy had slain and devoured. However, he at length valiantly resolved to issue forth and meet his fate. Meanwhile, the bee had acquitted himself of his toils and, posted securely at some distance, was employed in cleansing his wings and disengaging them from the ragged remnants of the cobweb. By this time the spider was adventured out, when beholding the chasms and ruins and dilapidations of his fortress, he was very near at his wits' end: he stormed and swore like a madman, and swelled till he was ready to burst. At length, casting his eye upon the bee and wisely gathering causes from events (for they knew each other by sight), "A plague split you," said he, "for a giddy son of a whore. Is it you, with a vengeance, that have made this litter here? Could you not look before you and be damned? Do you think I have nothing else to do (in the Devil's name) but to mend and repair after your arse?"

"Good words, friend," said the bee (having now pruned himself and being disposed to droll), "I'll give you my hand and word to come near your kennel no more. I was never in such a confounded pickle since I was born."

"Sirrah," replied the spider, "if it were not for breaking an old custom in our family never to stir abroad against an enemy, I should come and teach you better manners."

"I pray, have patience," said the bee, "or you will spend your substance – and, for aught I see, you may stand in need of it all – towards the repair of your house."

"Rogue, rogue," replied the spider. "Yet, methinks, you should have more respect to a person whom all the world allows to be so much your betters."*

"By my troth," said the bee, "the comparison will amount to a very good jest, and you will do me a favour: to let me know the reasons that all the world is pleased to use in so hopeful a dispute."

At this the spider, having swelled himself into the size and posture of a disputant, began his argument in the true spirit of controversy, with a resolution to be heartily scurrilous and angry, to urge on his own reasons without the least regard to the answers or objections of his opposite, and fully predetermined in his mind against all conviction.

"Not to disparage myself," said he, "by the comparison with such a rascal, what art thou but a vagabond without house or home, without stock or inheritance, born to no possession of your own but a pair of wings and a drone pipe? Your livelihood is a universal plunder upon nature, a free-booter over fields and gardens, and for the sake of stealing will rob a nettle as readily as a violet. Whereas I am a domestic animal, furnished with a native stock within myself. This large castle (to show my improvements in the mathematics)* is all built with my own hands, and the materials extracted altogether out of my own person."*

"I am glad," answered the bee, "to hear you grant at least that I am come honestly by my wings and my voice, for then, it seems, I am obliged to Heaven alone for my flights and my music, and Providence would never have bestowed on me two such gifts without designing them for the noblest ends. I visit, indeed, all the flowers and blossoms of the field and the garden, but whatever I collect from thence enriches myself, without the least injury to their beauty, their smell or their taste.* Now, for you and your skill in architecture and other mathematics, I have little to say: in that building of yours there might, for aught I know, have been labour and method enough, but by woeful experience for us both, 'tis too plain the materials are nought, and I hope you will henceforth take warning and consider duration and matter, as well as method and art. You boast, indeed, of being obliged to no other creature, but of drawing and spinning out all from yourself – that is to say, if we may judge of the liquor in the vessel by what issues out, you possess a good plentiful store of dirt and poison in your breast. And though I would by no means lessen or disparage your genuine stock of either, yet I doubt you are somewhat obliged for an increase of both to a little foreign assistance. Your inherent portion of dirt does not fail of acquisitions by sweepings exhaled from below, and one insect furnishes you with a share of poison to destroy another. So that, in short, the question comes to all this: whether is the nobler being of the two that which by a lazy contemplation of four inches round, by an overweening pride which, feeding and engendering on itself, turns all into excrement and venom, producing nothing at last but flybane and a cobweb, or that which, by a universal range, with long search, much study, true judgement and distinction of things, brings home honey and wax."

This dispute was managed with such eagerness, clamour and warmth that the two parties of books in arms below stood silent a while, waiting in suspense what would be the issue – which was not long undetermined, for the bee, grown impatient at so much loss of time, fled straight away to a bed of roses without looking for a reply and left the spider like an orator collected in himself and just prepared to burst out.

It happened upon this emergency that Aesop broke silence first. He had been of late most barbarously treated by a strange effect of the Regent's humanity, who had torn off his title page, sorely defaced one half of his leaves and chained him fast among a shelf of Moderns – where, soon discovering how high the quarrel was like to proceed, he tried all his arts and turned himself to a thousand forms.* At length, in the borrowed shape of an ass,* the Regent mistook him for a Modern, by which means he had time and opportunity to escape to the Ancients, just when the spider and the bee were entering into their contest – to which he gave his attention with a world of pleasure and, when it was ended, swore in the loudest key that in all his life he had never known two cases so parallel and adapt to each other as that in the window and this upon the shelves.

"The disputants," said he, "have admirably managed the dispute between them, have taken in the full strength of all that is to be said on both sides and exhausted the substance of every argument pro and con. It is but to adjust the reasonings of both to the present quarrel, then to compare and apply the labours and fruits of each, as the bee has learnedly deduced them, and we shall find the conclusion fall plain and close upon the Moderns and us. For, pray gentlemen, was ever anything so modern as the spider in his air, his turns and his paradoxes? He argues in the behalf of you his brethren and himself, with many boastings of his native stock and great genius, that he spins and spits wholly from himself, and scorns to own any obligation or assistance from without. Then he displays to you his great skill in architecture and improvement in the mathematics. To all this the bee, as an advocate retained by us the Ancients, thinks fit to answer that if one may judge of the great genius or inventions of the Moderns by what they have produced, you will hardly have countenance to bear you out in boasting of either. Erect your schemes with as much method and skill as you please – yet, if the materials be nothing but dirt spun out of your own entrails (the guts of Modern brains), the edifice will conclude at last in a cobweb, the duration of which, like that of other spiders' webs, may be imputed to their being forgotten or neglected or hid in a corner. For anything else of genuine that the Moderns may pretend to, I cannot recollect, unless it be a large vein of wrangling and satire,* much of a nature and substance with the spider's poison – which, however they pretend to spit wholly out of themselves, is improved by the same arts by feeding upon the insects and vermin of the age. As for us, the Ancients, we are content with the bee to pretend to nothing of our own beyond our wings and our voice – that is to say, our flights and our language. For the rest, whatever we have got has been by infinite labour and search and ranging through every corner of nature. The difference is that, instead of dirt and poison, we have rather chose to fill our hives with honey and wax, thus furnishing mankind with the two noblest of things, which are sweetness and light."

'Tis wonderful to conceive the tumult arisen among the books upon the close of this long descant of Aesop. Both parties took the hint, and heightened their animosities so on a sudden that they resolved it should come to a battle. Immediately, the two main bodies withdrew under their several ensigns to the farther parts of the library, and there entered into cabals and consults upon the present emergency. The Moderns were in very warm debates upon the choice of their leaders, and nothing less than the fear impending from their enemies could have kept them from mutinies upon this occasion. The difference was greatest among the horse, where every private trooper pretended to the chief command, from Tasso* and Milton to Dryden and Withers. The light-horse were commanded by Cowley and Despréaux.* There came the bowmen under their valiant leaders, Descartes, Gassendi and Hobbes,* whose strength was such that they could shoot their arrows beyond the atmosphere, never to fall down again but turn like that of Evander* into meteors, or like the cannonball into stars. Paracelsus brought a squadron of stink-pot flingers* from the snowy mountains of Raetia. There came a vast body of dragoons of different nations, under the leading of Harvey,* their great Aga – part armed with scythes, the weapons of death, part with lances and long knives, all steeped in poison, part shot bullets of a most malignant nature – and used white powder which infallibly killed without report.* There came several bodies of heavy-armed foot, all mercenaries, under the ensigns of Guicciardini, Davila, Polydore Vergil, Buchanan, Mariana, Camden* and others. The engineers were commanded by Regiomontanus and Wilkins.* The rest were a confused multitude, led by Scotus, Aquinas and Bellarmino,* of mighty bulk and stature, but without either arms, courage or discipline. In the last place came infinite swarms of *calones*,* a disorderly rout led by

L'Estrange,* rogues and ragamuffins that follow the camp for nothing but the plunder, all without coats to cover them.

The army of the Ancients was much fewer in number: Homer led the horse and Pindar the light-horse, Euclid was chief engineer, Plato and Aristotle commanded the bowmen, Herodotus and Livy the foot, Hippocrates the dragoons. The allies, led by Vossius* and Temple, brought up the rear.

All things violently tending to a decisive battle, Fame – who much frequented and had a large apartment formerly assigned her in the Regal Library – fled up straight to Jupiter, to whom she delivered a faithful account of all that passed between the two parties below (for, among the Gods, she always tells the truth).

Jove, in great concern, convokes a council in the Milky Way. The Senate assembled, he declares the occasion of convening them: a bloody battle just impendent between two mighty armies of ancient and modern creatures, called books, wherein the celestial interest was but too deeply concerned. Momus, the patron of the Moderns,* made an excellent speech in their favour, which was answered by Pallas, the protectress of the Ancients. The assembly was divided in their affections, when Jupiter commanded the Book of Fate to be laid before him. Immediately were brought by Mercury three large volumes in folio, containing memoirs of all things past, present and to come.* The clasps were of silver, double gilt, the covers of celestial turkey leather and the paper such as here on earth might almost pass for vellum. Jupiter, having silently read the decree, would communicate the import to none, but presently shut up the book.

Without the doors of this assembly, there attended a vast number of light, nimble gods, menial servants to Jupiter:* these are his ministering instruments in all affairs below. They travel in a caravan, more or less together, and are fastened to each other like a link of galley slaves by a light chain, which passes from them to Jupiter's great toe — and yet, in receiving or delivering a message, they may never approach above the lowest step of his throne, where he and they whisper to each other through a long hollow trunk. These deities are called by mortal men accidents, or events, but the Gods call them second causes. Jupiter having delivered his message to a certain number of these divinities, they flew immediately down to the pinnacle of the Regal Library and, consulting a few minutes, entered unseen and disposed the parties according to their orders.

Meanwhile Momus, fearing the worst and calling to mind an ancient prophecy which bore no very good face to his children the Moderns, bent his flight to the region of a malignant deity called Criticism. She dwelt on the top of a snowy mountain in Nova Zembla: there Momus found her extended in her den, upon the spoils of numberless volumes half-devoured. At her right hand sat Ignorance,* her father and husband blind with age; at her left Pride, her mother, dressing her up in the scraps of paper herself had torn. There was Opinion her sister, light of foot, hoodwinked and headstrong, yet giddy and perpetually turning. About her played her children, Noise and Impudence, Dullness and Vanity, Positiveness, Pedantry and Ill Manners. The goddess herself had claws like a cat: her head and ears and voice resembled those of an ass, her teeth fallen out before, her eyes turned inward, as if she looked only upon herself. Her diet was the overflowing of her own gall: her spleen was so large as to stand prominent like a dug of the first rate, nor wanted excrescencies in form of teats, at which a crew of ugly monsters were greedily sucking – and, what is wonderful to conceive, the bulk of spleen increased faster than the sucking could diminish it.

"Goddess," said Momus, "can you sit idly here, while our devout worshippers, the Moderns, are this minute entering into a cruel battle and, perhaps, now lying under the swords of their enemies? Who then, hereafter, will ever sacrifice or build altars to our divinities?* Haste therefore to the British Isle and, if possible, prevent their destruction while I make factions among the gods and gain them over to our party."

Momus, having thus delivered himself, stayed not for an answer,* but left the goddess to her own resentment. Up she rose in a rage, and as it is the form upon such occasions, began a soliloquy.

"'Tis I," said she, "who give wisdom to infants and idiots. By me children grow wiser than their parents. By me beaux become politicians and schoolboys judges of philosophy.* By me sophisters debate and conclude upon the depths of knowledge, and coffee-house wits, instinct by me, can correct an author's style and display his minutest errors without understanding a syllable of his matter or his language. By me striplings spend their judgement as they do their estate before it comes into their hands. 'Tis I who have deposed wit and knowledge from their empire over poetry and advanced myself in their stead. And shall a few upstart Ancients dare to oppose me? But come, my aged parents, and you, my children dear, and thou my beauteous sister – let us ascend my chariot and haste to assist our devout Moderns, who are now sacrificing to us a hecatomb, as I perceive by that grateful smell which from thence reaches my nostrils."

The goddess and her train, having mounted the chariot, which was drawn by tame geese, flew over infinite regions, shedding her influence in due places, till at length she arrived at her beloved island of Britain. But in hovering over its metropolis, what blessings did she not let fall upon her seminaries of Gresham and Covent Garden?* And now she reached the fatal plain of St James's Library, at what time the two armies were upon the point to engage – where, entering with all her caravan unseen and landing upon a case of shelves now deserted, but once inhabited by a colony of virtuosi, she stayed awhile to observe the posture of both armies.

But here the tender cares of a mother began to fill her thoughts and move in her breast. For, at the head of a troop of Modern bowmen, she cast her eyes upon her son Wotton, to whom the Fates had assigned a very short thread – Wotton, a young hero whom an unknown father of mortal race begot by stolen embraces with this goddess. He was the darling of his mother, above all her children, and she resolved to go and comfort him. But first, according to the good old custom of deities, she cast about to change her shape, for fear the divinity of her countenance might dazzle his mortal sight and overcharge the rest of his senses. She therefore gathered up her person into an octavo compass:* her body grew white and arid and split into pieces with dryness; the thick turned into pasteboard, and the thin into paper, upon which her parents and children artfully strewed a black juice, or decoction of gall and soot, in form of letters; her head and voice and spleen kept their primitive form, and that which before was a cover of skin did still continue so. In which guise she marched on towards the Moderns, undistinguishable in shape and dress from the divine Bentley, Wotton's dearest friend.

"Brave Wotton," said the goddess, "why do our troops stand idle here, to spend their present vigour and opportunity of this day? Away, let us haste to the generals and advise to give the onset immediately." Having spoke thus, she took the ugliest of her monsters, full-glutted from her spleen, and flung it invisibly into his mouth – which, flying straight up into his head, squeezed out his eyeballs, gave him a distorted look and half-overturned his brain. Then she privately ordered two of her beloved children, Dullness and Ill Manners, closely to attend his person in all encounters. Having thus accoutred him, she vanished in a mist,* and the hero perceived it was the goddess, his mother.

The destined hour of fate being now arrived, the fight began – whereof, before I dare adventure to make a particular description, I must, after the example of other authors, petition for a hundred tongues and mouths and hands and pens,* which would all be too little to perform so immense a work. Say, Goddess that presidest over history, who it was that first advanced in the field of battle. Paracelsus, at the head of his dragoons, observing Galen* in the adverse wing, darted his javelin with a mighty force, which the brave Ancient received upon his shield, the point breaking in the second fold.  *   *   *

*Hic pauca desunt.*
                *   *   *   *   *   *   *   *

                *   *   *   *   *   *   *   *

They bore the wounded Aga on their shields to his chariot.  *   *   *   *   *   *

            *   *   *   *   *   *   *   *

*Desunt nonnulla.*
            *   *   *   *   *   *   *   *

            *   *   *   *   *   *   *   *

            *   *   *   *   *   *   *   *

Then Aristotle, observing Bacon* advance with a furious mien, drew his bow to the head and let fly his arrow, which missed the valiant Modern and went hizzing over his head, but Descartes it hit: the steel point quickly found a defect in his headpiece, it pierced the leather and the pasteboard and went in at his right eye. The torture of the pain whirled the valiant bowman round, till death, like a star of superior influence, drew him into his own vortex.*  *  *  *

\*  \*  \*  \*  \*  \*  \*  \*  \*  *Ingens hiatus*

\*  \*  \*  \*  \*  \*  \*  \*  \*  *hic in MS.**

\*  \*  \*  \*  \*  \*  \*  \*  \*

when Homer appeared at the head of the cavalry mounted on a furious horse, with difficulty managed by the rider himself, but which no other mortal durst approach. He rode among the enemy's ranks and bore down all before him. Say, Goddess, whom he slew first and whom he slew last. First, *Gondibert*\* advanced against him, clad in heavy armour and mounted on a staid sober gelding, not so famed for his speed as his docility in kneeling\* whenever his rider would mount or alight. He had made a vow to Pallas that he would never leave the field till he had spoilt Homer of his armour – madman, who had never once

*Vid. Homer.*\* seen the wearer nor understood his strength. Him Homer overthrew, horse and man to the ground, there to be trampled and choked in the dirt. Then, with a long spear, he slew Denham,\* a stout Modern, who from his father's side derived his lineage from Apollo, but his mother was of mortal race. He fell and bit the earth. The celestial part Apollo took and made it a star, but the terrestrial lay wallowing upon the ground. Then Homer slew Wesley* with a kick of his horse's heel; he took Perrault by mighty force out of his saddle, then hurled him at Fontenelle,* with the same blow dashing out both their brains.

On the left wing of the horse, Virgil appeared in shining armour, completely fitted to his body; he was mounted on a dapple-grey steed, the slowness of whose pace was an effect of the highest mettle and vigour. He cast his eye on the adverse wing, with a desire to find an object worthy of his valour – when, behold, upon a sorrel gelding of a monstrous size appeared a foe, issuing from among the thickest of the enemy's squadrons. But his speed was less than his noise, for his horse, old and lean, spent the dregs of his strength in a high trot, which though it made slow advances, yet caused a loud clashing of his armour, terrible to hear. The two cavaliers had now approached within the throw of a lance, when the stranger desired a parley and, lifting up the vizard of his helmet, a face hardly appeared from within, which after a pause was known for that of the renowned Dryden. The brave Ancient suddenly started as one possessed with surprise and disappointment together, for the helmet was nine times too large for the head – which appeared situate far in the hinder part, even like the lady in a lobster,* or like a mouse under a canopy of state, or like a shrivelled beau from within the penthouse of a modern periwig – and the voice was suited to the visage, sounding weak and remote. Dryden, in a long harangue, soothed up the good Ancient, called him Father and, by a large deduction of genealogies, made it plainly appear that they were nearly related.[*] Then he humbly proposed an exchange of armour as a lasting mark of hospitality between them. Virgil consented (for the goddess Diffidence came unseen and cast a mist before his eyes), though his was of gold and cost a hundred beeves, the others but of rusty iron.[*] *Vid. Homer.* However, this glittering armour became the Modern yet worse than his own. Then they agreed to exchange horses, but when it came to the trial, Dryden was afraid and utterly unable to mount.   &ast;   &ast;   &ast;   &ast;   &ast;

&ast;   &ast;   &ast;   &ast;   &ast;   &ast;   &ast;   &ast;

*Alter hiatus in MS.*&ast;   &ast;   &ast;   &ast;   &ast;   &ast;   &ast;   &ast;   &ast;

&ast;   &ast;   &ast;   &ast;   &ast;   &ast;   &ast;   &ast;

Lucan appeared upon a fiery horse, of admirable shape but headstrong, bearing the rider where he list, over the field. He made a mighty slaughter among the enemy's horse – which destruction to stop, Blackmore,&ast; a famous Modern (but one of the mercenaries), strenuously opposed himself and darted a javelin with a strong hand which, falling short of its mark, struck deep in the earth. Then Lucan threw a lance, but Aesculapius&ast; came, unseen, and turned off the point.

"Brave Modern," said Lucan, "I perceive some god protects you, for never did my arm so deceive me before, but what mortal can contend with a god? Therefore, let us fight no longer, but present gifts to each other." Lucan then bestowed the Modern a pair of spurs, and Blackmore gave Lucan a bridle.

\* \* \* \* \* \* \* \*     *Pauca*
                                                     *desunt.*\*
\* \* \* \* \* \* \* \*

Creech.\* But the goddess Dullness took a cloud, formed it into the shape of Horace, armed and mounted, and placed it in a flying posture before him. Glad was the cavalier to begin a combat with a flying foe, and pursued the image threatening loud, till at last it led him to the peaceful bower his father Ogilby,\* by whom he was disarmed and assigned to his repose.

Then Pindar slew —⸻— and —⸻— and Oldham\* and —⸻— and Aphra the

— 63 —

Amazon, light of foot.* Never advancing in a direct line,* but wheeling with incredible agility and force, he made a terrible slaughter among the enemy's light-horse. Him, when Cowley observed, his generous heart burned within him, and he advanced against the fierce Ancient, imitating his address and pace and career, as well as the vigour of his horse and his own skill would allow. When the two cavaliers had approached within the length of three javelins, first Cowley threw a lance, which missed Pindar and, passing into the enemy's ranks, fell ineffectual to the ground, then Pindar darted a javelin so large and weighty that scarce a dozen cavaliers, as cavaliers are in our degenerate days,* could raise it from the ground. Yet he threw it with ease, and it went by an unerring hand, singing through the air, nor could the Modern have avoided present death if he had not luckily opposed the shield that had been given him by Venus.* And now both heroes drew their swords, but the Modern was so aghast and disordered that he knew not where he was. His shield dropped from his hands: thrice he fled, and thrice he could not escape. At last he turned and, lifting up his hands, in the posture of a suppliant: "Godlike Pindar," said he, "spare my life, and possess my horse with these arms, besides the ransom which my friends will give when they hear I am alive and your prisoner."

"Dog," said Pindar, "let your ransom stay with your friends, but your carcass shall be left for the fowls of the air and the beasts of the field."* With that, he raised his sword and, with a mighty stroke, cleft the wretched Modern in twain, the sword pursuing the blow, and one half lay panting on the ground to be trod in pieces by the horses' feet, the other half was borne by the frighted steed through the field. This Venus took and washed it seven times in ambrosia, then struck it thrice with a sprig of amaranth – upon which, the leather grew round and soft, the leaves turned into feathers and, being gilded before, continued gilded still. So it became a dove, and she harnessed it to her chariot.* *  *  *  *

\*  \*  \*  \*  \*  \*  \*  \*

*Hiatus valde deflendus in MS.**    \*  \*  \*  \*  \*  \*  \*  \*

\*  \*  \*  \*  \*  \*  \*  \*

Day being far spent and the numerous *The Episode of Bentley and Wotton.* forces of the Moderns half-inclining to a retreat, there issued forth from a squadron of their heavy-armed foot a captain whose name was Bentley, in person the most deformed of all the Moderns: tall but without shape or comeliness, large but without strength or proportion. His armour was patched up of a thousand incoherent pieces,* and the sound of it, as he marched, was loud and dry, like that made by the fall of a sheet of lead which an Etesian wind* blows suddenly down from the roof of some steeple. His helmet was of old rusty iron, but the vizard was brass, which – tainted by his breath – corrupted into copperas, not wanted gall from the same fountain, so that, whenever provoked by anger or labour, an atramentous quality of most malignant nature was seen to distil from his lips. In his right hand he grasped a flail and – that he might never be unprovided of an offensive weapon – a vessel full of ordure in his left.* Thus, completely armed, he advanced with a slow and heavy pace, where the Modern chiefs were holding a consult upon the sum of things – who, as he came onwards, laughed to behold his crooked leg and hump shoulder, which his boot and armour vainly endeavouring to hide, were forced to comply with and expose. The generals made use of him for his talent of railing which, kept within government, proved frequently of great service to their cause, but at other times did more mischief than good, for at the least touch of offence, and often without any at all, he would, like a wounded elephant, convert it against his leaders.* Such, at this juncture, was the disposition of Bentley: grieved to see the enemy prevail and dissatisfied with everybody's conduct but his own. He humbly gave the Modern generals to understand that he conceived, with great submission, they were all a pack of rogues and fools and sons of whores and damned cowards and confounded loggerheads and illiterate whelps and nonsensical scoundrels; that if himself had been constituted general, those presumptuous dogs, the Ancients, would long before this have *Vid. Homer de Thersite.* been beaten out of the field.*

"You," said he, "sit here idle, but when I, or any other valiant Modern, kill an enemy, you are sure to seize the spoil. But I will not march one foot against the foe till you all swear to me that, whomever I take or kill, his arms I shall quietly possess." Bentley having spoke thus, Scaliger,* bestowing him a sour look: "Miscreant prater," said he, "eloquent only in thine own eyes, thou railest without wit or truth or discretion, the malignity of thy temper perverteth nature, thy learning makes thee more barbarous, thy study of humanity* more inhuman, thy converse amongst poets more grovelling, miry and dull. All arts of civilizing others render thee rude and intractable; courts have taught thee ill manners, and polite conversation has finished thee a pedant. Besides, a greater coward burdeneth not the army. But never despond, I pass my word, whatever spoil thou takest shall certainly be thy own, though I hope that vile carcass will first become a prey to kites and worms."

Bentley durst not reply but, half-choked with spleen and rage, withdrew, in full resolution of performing some great achievement. With him, for his aid and companion, he took his beloved Wotton, resolving by policy or surprise to attempt some neglected quarter of the Ancients' army. They began their march over carcasses of their slaughtered friends, then to the right of their own forces, then wheeled northward, till they came to Aldrovandus's tomb,* which they passed on the side of the declining sun. And now they arrived with fear towards the enemy's out-guards, looking about if haply they might spy the quarters of the wounded or some straggling sleepers, unarmed and remote from the rest. As when two mongrel curs whom native greediness and domestic want provoke and join in partnership, though fearful, nightly to invade the folds of some rich grazier, they, with tails depressed and lolling tongues, creep soft and slow. Meanwhile, the conscious moon, now in her zenith on their guilty heads, darts perpendicular rays – nor dare they bark, though much provoked at her refulgent visage, whether seen in puddle by reflection or in sphere direct, but one surveys the region round, while t'other scouts the plain if haply to discover at distance from the flock some carcass half-devoured, the refuse of gorged wolves or ominous ravens. So marched this lovely, loving pair of friends, nor with less fear and circumspection, when at distance they might perceive two shining suits of armour hanging upon an oak, and the owners not far off in a profound sleep. The two friends drew lots, and the pursuing of this adventure fell to Bentley. On he went, and in his van Confusion and Amaze, while Horror and Affright brought up the rear. As he came near, behold two heroes of the Ancients' army, Phalaris and Aesop, lay fast asleep. Bentley would fain have dispatched them both and, stealing close, aimed his flail at Phalaris's breast. But then the goddess Affright, interposing, caught the Modern in her icy arms and dragged him from the danger she foresaw, for both the dormant heroes happened to turn at the same instant, though soundly sleeping and busy in a dream. For Phalaris was just that minute dreaming how a most vile poetaster had lampooned him, and how he had got him roaring in his bull,* and Aesop dreamt that, as he and the ancient chiefs were lying on the ground, a wild ass broke loose, ran about trampling and kicking and dunging in their faces.* Bentley, leaving the two heroes asleep, seized on both their armours and withdrew in quest of his darling Wotton.

He, in the meantime, had wandered long in search of some enterprise, till at length he arrived at a small rivulet that issued from a fountain hard by called, in the language of mortal men, Helicon. Here he stopped and, parched with thirst, resolved to allay it in this limpid stream. Thrice, with profane hands, he essayed to raise the water to his lips, and thrice it slipped all through his fingers. Then he stooped prone on his breast, but ere his mouth had kissed the liquid crystal, Apollo came and, in the channel, held his shield betwixt the Modern and the fountain, so that he drew up nothing but mud. For although no fountain on earth can compare with the clearness of Helicon, yet there lies at bottom a thick sediment of slime and mud, for so Apollo begged of Jupiter as a punishment to those who durst attempt to taste it with unhallowed lips, and for a lesson to all not to draw too deep or far from the spring.*

At the fountainhead, Wotton discerned two heroes: the one he could not distinguish,* but the other was soon known for Temple, general of the allies to the Ancients. His back was turned, and he was employed in drinking large draughts in his helmet from the fountain, where he had withdrawn himself to rest from the toils of the war. Wotton, observing him, with quaking knees and trembling hands spoke thus to himself:

*Vid. Homer.*  "Oh, that I could kill this destroyer of our army, what renown should I purchase among the chiefs! But to issue out against him, man for man, shield against shield and lance against lance, what Modern of us dare? For he fights like a god, and Pallas or Apollo are ever at his elbow. But oh, Mother,* if what Fame reports be true, that I am the son of so great a goddess, grant me to hit Temple with this lance, that the stroke may send him to Hell and that I may return in safety and triumph, laden with his spoils!" The first part of his prayer the Gods granted, at the intercession of his mother and of Momus, but the rest, by a perverse wind sent from Fate, was scattered in the air.* Then Wotton grasped his lance and, brandishing it thrice over his head, darted it with all his might, the goddess his mother at the same time adding strength to his arm. Away the lance went hizzing, and reached even to the belt of the averted Ancient, upon which, lightly grazing, it fell to the ground. Temple neither felt the weapon touch him nor heard it fall, and Wotton might have escaped to his army with the honour of having remitted his lance against so great a leader

unrevenged, but Apollo, enraged that a javelin flung by the assistance of so foul a goddess
should pollute his fountain, put on the shape
of ————* and softly came to young Boyle,
who then accompanied Temple. He pointed
first to the lance, then to the distant Modern
that flung it, and commanded the young hero
to take immediate revenge.* Boyle, clad in a
suit of armour which had been given him by
all the gods, immediately advanced against
the trembling foe, who now fled before him.
As a young lion in the Libyan plains or Araby
desert sent by his aged sire to hunt for prey or
health or exercise, he scours along, wishing
to meet some tiger from the mountains or a
furious boar. If chance a wild ass, with bray-
ings importune, affronts his ear, the generous

beast, though loathing to distain his claws with blood so vile, yet much provoked at the offensive noise – which Echo, foolish nymph, like her ill-judging sex, repeats much louder, and with more delight than Philomela's song* – he vindicates the honour of the forest and hunts the noisy, long-eared animal. So Wotton fled, so Boyle pursued. But Wotton, heavy-armed and slow of foot, began to slack his course, when his lover Bentley appeared, returning laden with the spoils of the two sleeping Ancients. Boyle observed him well and, soon discovering the helmet and shield of Phalaris his friend, both which he had lately with his own hands new polished and gilded, rage sparkled in his eyes and, leaving his pursuit after Wotton, he furiously rushed

*Vid. Homer.* on against this new approacher. Fain would he be revenged on both, but both now fled different ways.* And as a woman in a little house that gets a painful livelihood by spinning, if chance her geese be scattered o'er the common, she courses round the plain from side to side compelling here and there the stragglers to the flock, they cackle loud and flutter o'er the champaign, so Boyle pursued, so fled this pair of friends. Finding at length their flight was vain, they bravely joined and drew themselves in phalanx. First, Bentley threw a spear with all his force,* hoping to pierce the enemy's breast, but Pallas came unseen and in the air took off the point and clapped on one of lead – which, after a dead bang against the enemy's shield, fell blunted to the ground. Then Boyle, observing well his time, took a lance of wondrous length and sharpness and, as this pair of friends compacted stood close side to side, he wheeled him to the right and, with unusual force, darted the weapon.* Bentley saw his fate approach and, flanking down his arms close to his ribs hoping to save his body, in went the point, passing through arm and side, nor stopped or spent its force till it had also pierced the valiant Wotton who, going to sustain his dying friend, shared his fate. As when a skilful cook has trussed a brace of woodcocks he, with iron skewer, pierces the tender sides of both, their legs and wings close pinioned to their ribs, so was this pair of friends transfixed, till down they fell, joined in their lives, joined in their deaths – so closely joined that Charon would mistake them both for one and waft them over Styx for half his fare. Farewell, beloved, loving pair. Few equals have you left behind, and happy and immortal shall you be if all my wit and eloquence can make you.

And now  *   *   *   *   *   *
 *   *   *   *   *   *   *   *
 *   *   *   *   *   *   *   *

*Desunt cætera.*

FINIS

# Note on the Text

The text is based on the first and fifth editions of 1704 and 1710, both published in London by John Nutt. The fifth edition included a set of previously unpublished footnotes, purportedly commissioned by the editor, but likely to have been written by Swift himself. These are marked "Note to the fifth edition". A further set of notes written by William Pate, which appeared in the 1808 edition of Swift's *Works*, are marked "MS Pate". Errors have been silently corrected, and the spelling and punctuation have been standardized, modernized and made consistent throughout.

# Notes

p. 4, *The controversy… voluminously, rejoined*: Sir William Temple (1628–99), diplomat and author, introduced the ancient-versus-modern controversy to England with his essay 'Of Ancient and Modern Learning' (1690), which came down on the side of the ancients. The young Swift served as Temple's secretary and helped to prepare many of his later works for publication. William Wotton (1666–1727), linguist and theologian, argued in his *Reflections upon Ancient and Modern Learning* (1694) that the moderns' superiority in algebra and geometry was responsible for huge advances in architecture and technology. Richard Bentley (1662–1742), philologist and classical scholar, later master of Trinity College, Cambridge, had been appointed keeper of the King's libraries in 1693. Like the majority of his Cambridge colleagues, Bentley was a staunch defender of the moderns. This passage refers to Sir William Temple's essay of 1690, the second edition of W. Wotton's *Reflections*, Dr Bentley's 'Dissertations upon the Epistles of Phalaris… and the Fables of Aesop' which was contained in the appendix of Wotton's book, Charles Boyle's edition of the *Epistles of Phalaris* (1695) and his 'Dr Bentley's Dissertations… Examined by Charles

Boyle, Esq.' (1698) and Bentley's 'Dissertation upon the Epistles of Phalaris. With an Answer to the Objections of the Honourable Charles Boyle, Esquire' (1699). Charles Boyle (1674–1731) was the fourth Earl of Orrery.

p. 9, *the annual records… riches*: Riches produceth pride; pride is war's ground, etc. *Vid. Ephem. de* Mary Clarke; *opt. Edit.* (Note to fifth edition.) "*Ephem. de* Mary Clarke" refers to Wing's sheet almanac, established by the astronomer and astrologer Vincent Wing (1619–68), and continued by his nephew John Wing. It was printed by Mary Clarke, and bore the quoted phrases as part of its inscription. "*Opt. Edit.*" is an abbreviation of the Latin *optima editio* (literally, best edition), and refers the reader to the current edition of the almanac.

p. 10, *the phrase of writers upon the politics*: See *Leviathan* II, 17, in which Thomas Hobbes (1588–1679) discusses Aristotle's categorization of bees and ants as "political creatures".

p. 13, *the east*: Whence we derive all learning (MS Pate).

p. 14, *summity*: An archaic form of "summit".

p. 16, *this difference broke out... war*: The quarrel over the relative merits of ancient and modern culture was current in Britain and France during the 1690s.

p. 17, *set up trophies on both sides*: See Thucydides I, 54, in which the Corinthians and Corcyraeans both set up trophies proclaiming themselves the victors of their recent skirmish.

p. 17, *happily revived of late*: Possibly a reference to Catholic celebrations of the Battle of the Boyne (1690).

p. 18, *their representatives*: Their title pages. (Note to fifth edition.)

p. 18, *In these books... while he is alive*: See Milton, *Areopagitica* II: "Books [...] do preserve as in a vial the purest efficacy and extraction of that living intellect that bred them."

p. 18, *inform them*: Imbue them with his spirit.

p. 19, *some philosophers... hominis*: See Thomas Vaughan (1621–66), *Anthroposophia Theomagica*: "For that part of man which Paracelsus calls *homo sydereus*, and more appositely *brutum hominis* [...]

hovers sometimes about the dormitories of the dead."

p. 19, *for fear of mutual violence... chains*: The practice of chaining valuable books in libraries continued into the mid-eighteenth century.

p. 20, *Of which invention... years*: By the time of Duns Scotus (*c.*1265–1308), Plato had long since been supplanted by Aristotle.

p. 22, *The Guardian of the Regal Library*: Richard Bentley.

p. 22, *chiefly renowned for his humanity*: The Honourable Mr Boyle, in the preface to his edition of *Phalaris*, says he was refused a manuscript by the library-keeper, *pro solita humanitate sua*. (Note to fifth edition.) Boyle became a proponent of the ancients and produced a translation of the *Epistles of Phalaris* (1695). While working on this translation, Boyle had borrowed a manuscript for collation, but the collator failed to complete his task before Bentley, who was leaving London, requested the return of the manuscript. Boyle's preface to the *Epistles* accuses Bentley of thwarting his work: "*pro singulari sua humanitate*". Bentley referred to this passage in his 'Dissertation upon the Epistles of Phalaris' (1697), rendering the Latin, "out of his singular Humanity".

p. 22, *two of the Ancient chiefs*: Phalaris and Aesop. Bentley's 'Dissertation' of 1697 enraged the advocates for the ancients by challenging the authenticity of Phalaris's epistles. He went on to question the authorship of several other works, including Aesop's *Fables*.

p. 24, *strange confusion of place... library*: In his *Examination of Dr Bentley's Dissertations on the Epistles of Phalaris* (1698), Boyle accused Bentley of refusing another scholar permission to view a manuscript on the grounds that "the library was not fit to be seen". Bentley replied in his second 'Dissertation' (1699) that: "I will own that I have often said and lamented that the library was not fit to be seen. [...] If the room be too mean, and too little for the books; if it be much out of repair, if the situation be inconvenient; is the library-keeper to answer for it?"

p. 25, *Seven Wise Masters*: A famous cycle of stories also known as *The Seven Sages of Rome*.

p. 25, *Dryden*: John Dryden (1631–1700), one of the leading poets of the Restoration. He was an influential literary critic and translator, and was made Poet Laureate in 1667. Swift bore a grudge against Dryden for his remark that "Cousin Swift, you will never be a poet".

p. 25, *Withers*: George Wither (1588–1667), poet and satirical essayist, also commonly referred to as Withers. His early pastoral poems were well received, but his later work was highly politicized and deeply unpopular; by the end of the seventeenth century his name had become a byword for bad poetry.

p. 26, *the Moderns were... two*: According to the modern paradox. (Note to fifth edition.) See Francis Bacon, *Advancement of Learning* 1, 5, 1: "These times are the ancient times, when the world is ancient, and not those which we account ancient *ordine retrogrado*, by a computation backward from ourselves."

p. 29, *conversed*: I.e. conversant.

p. 29, *the modern way of fortification*: See Perrault's *Parallel Between Ancients and Moderns* (1688–92). Instigator of the feud between the ancients and the moderns in France, Charles Perrault (1628–1703) was a proponent of the moderns, and argued that they had surpassed the ancients in the art of fortification.

p. 31, *Beelzebub*: The Hebrew god of flies (MS Pate).

p. 33, *betters*: The plural form was commonly used to refer to a single person at this time.

p. 34, *to show my improvements in the mathematics*: It was often claimed that the moderns held sway over the ancients in the field of mathematics.

p. 34, *out of my own person*: See René Descartes, *Discourse on the Method of Rightly Conducting the Reason, and Seeking Truth in the Sciences*, Chapter 1: "As to the reason or sense […] I am disposed to believe that it is to be found complete in each individual."

p. 35, *I visit, indeed... taste*: See Temple's 'Of Poetry': "[Bees] must range through fields, as well as gardens, choose such flowers as they please, and by properties and scents they only know and distinguish: they must work up their cells with admirable art, extract their honey with infinite labour, and sever it from the wax with such distinction and choice as belongs to none but themselves to perform or to judge."

p. 38, *he tried all his arts... forms*: See Virgil, *Georgics* IV, 440–42.

p. 38, *ass*: In his 'Dissertation', Bentley quoted the Greek proverb, "Leucon carries one thing, and his ass quite another". Boyle interpreted this as a personal attack and complained in his *Examination* that Bentley had called him an ass.

p. 41, *a large vein of wrangling and satire*: See Temple, 'Of Ancient and Modern Learning': "I wish the vein of ridiculing all that is serious and good, all honour and virtue as well as learning and piety, may have no worse effects on any other state."

p. 43, *Tasso*: Torquato Tasso (1544–95), Italian lyric poet.

p. 43, *Cowley and Despréaux*: The poet Abraham Cowley (1618–67) and the French poet and critic

Nicolas Boileau-Despréaux (1636–1711), more commonly known as Boileau.

p. 43, *Descartes, Gassendi and Hobbes*: The French philosopher Pierre Gassendi (1592–1655), named here with Descartes (1596–1650) and Hobbes (1588–1679) to provide a broad cross section of modern philosophers.

p. 43, *like that of Evander*: An error on Swift's part: the reference is to Acestes in the *Aeneid* v, 525–28.

p. 43, *Paracelsus brought a squadron of stink-pot flingers*: Paracelsus, born Philippus von Hohenheim (1493–1541), was a Swiss Renaissance physician, botanist, alchemist and astrologer, often referred to as the father of toxicology. He put forward the view that all substances are toxic if taken in great quantities, but safe if taken in small doses.

p. 44, *dragoons… Harvey*: In Swift's army of the Moderns, the dragoons are writers of medical tracts. William Harvey (1578–1657) was the physician who discovered the circulation of the blood – a fact called into question in Temple's 'Of Ancient and Modern Learning'.

p. 44, *white powder which… report*: See Sir Thomas Browne, *Vulgar Errors* ii, 5, 5: "Of white powder and such as is discharged without report, there is no small noise in the world." See also John Cleveland, *Rupertismus* 39–40: "For beauty, like white powder, makes no noise, / and yet the silent hypocrite destroys."

p. 44, *Guicciardini… Camden*: Francesco Guicciardini (1483–1540) was an Italian historian and statesman, often considered the father of modern history. Enrico Caterino Davila (1576–1631) was an Italian historian and diplomat. Polydore Vergil (c.1470–1555) was an Italian historian, otherwise known as P.V. Castellensis. George Buchanan (1506–82) was a Scottish historian and humanist scholar. Juan de Mariana (1536–1624), also known as Father Mariana, was a Spanish historian, scholastic and Jesuit priest. William Camden (1551–1623) was an English historian and herald.

p. 44, *Regiomontanus and Wilkins*: Johannes Müller von Königsberg (1436–76) – known as Regiomontanus – was a German mathematician and astronomer. John Wilkins (1614–72) was a theologian, natural philosopher and founder member of the Royal Society. He was referred to scathingly by Temple in his 'Thoughts upon Reviewing the Essay of Ancient and Modern Learning' and praised by Bentley in his second 'Dissertation' of 1699.

p. 44, *Bellarmino*: Roberto Francesco Romolo Bellarmino (1542–1621), Italian Jesuit and cardinal of the Catholic Church.

p. 44, *calones*: These are pamphlets, which are not bound or covered. (Note to fifth edition.) "*Calones*" were slaves who performed menial tasks for the camp and its officers.

p. 45, *L'Estrange*: Sir Roger L'Estrange (1616–1704), propagandist and press censor. In the months leading up to and immediately following the Restoration, L'Estrange wrote a number of royalist pamphlets; after the coronation of Charles II, he acted as an informer on illegal anti-government printing and bookselling.

p. 45, *Vossius*: Either Gerrit Janszoon Vos, commonly known by his Latin name, Gerardus Vossius (1577–1649), or, more likely, his son Isaak Vossius

(1618–89), a scholar and manuscript-collector who amassed what was held to be the best private library in the world. Swift read his *De Sibyllinis* in 1698.

p. 46, *Momus, the patron of the Moderns*: Momus, Greek god of mockery and censure, is the archetypal carping critic. See Swift, *A Tale of a Tub* III: "Every true critic is a hero born, descending in a direct line from a celestial stem, by Momus and Hybris."

p. 46, *all things past, present and to come*: See *Iliad* I, 70.

p. 47, *Without the doors... Jupiter*: See *Iliad* VIII, 19.

p. 48, *At her right hand sat Ignorance*: See Temple, 'Of Ancient and Modern Learning': "His pride is greater than his ignorance; and what he wants in knowledge, he supplies by sufficiency."

p. 50, *Who then, hereafter... divinities*: See *Aeneid* I, 48–49.

p. 50, *stayed not for an answer*: See Bacon, 'On Truth': "What is truth? said jesting Pilate; and would not stay for an answer."

p. 51, *By me children grow... philosophy*: See Temple, 'Of Ancient and Modern Learning': "A boy of fifteen is wiser than his father at forty, the meanest subject than his prince or governors; and the modern scholars, because they have for a hundred years learnt their lesson pretty well, are much more knowing than the ancients their masters."

p. 52, *Gresham and Covent Garden*: Gresham College was the meeting place of the Royal Society; Covent Garden was the site of Will's Coffee House, favoured meeting place of poets and wits.

p. 54, *an octavo compass*: The second edition of Wotton's *Reflections* was published in octavo with Bentley's 'Dissertation' (1697).

p. 55, *she vanished in a mist*: See *Aeneid* i, 412.

p. 56, *petition for a hundred... pens*: See *Aeneid* vi, 625.

p. 56, *Paracelsus... Galen*: See Temple, 'Thoughts upon Reviewing the Essay of Ancient and Modern Learning' (1701): "Till the new philosophy had gotten ground in these parts of the world, which is about fifty or sixty years' date, there were but few that ever pretended to exceed the ancients; those that did were only some physicians, as Paracelsus and his disciples, who introduced new notions in physic and new methods of practice in opposition to the Galenical." Aelius Galenus (129–*c*.217), better known as Galen of Pergamon, was one of the foremost physicians and medical scholars of antiquity.

p. 56, *Hic pauca desunt*: "Here a few lines are missing" (Latin).

p. 56, *Desunt nonnulla*: "A little is missing" (Latin).

p. 57, *Bacon*: In his 'Of Ancient and Modern Learning', Temple had named Bacon (1561–1626) as one of the greatest of the moderns; here as elsewhere Swift appears to follow Temple's lead.

p. 57, *drew him into his own vortex*: A reference to Descartes's theory of vortices.

p. 57, *Ingens hiatus hic in MS*: "Here there is a large lacuna in the MS" (Latin).

p. 58, *Gondibert*: Sir William Davenant (MS Pate). *Gondibert* an epic poem by Sir William Davenant

(1606–68), had been highly praised by contemporary critics, but was thought by Temple to be overrated.

p. 58, *not so famed... kneeling*: See *Hudibras* I, 1, 437–40.

p. 58, *Vid. Homer*: "See Homer" (Latin).

p. 58, *Denham*: Sir John Denham's poems are very unequal, extremely good and very indifferent, so that his detractors said he was not the real author of 'Cooper's Hill'. (Note to fifth edition.) See 'The Session of the Poets' in *Poems on Affairs of State*, vol. I (ed. 1699, p. 210): "Then in came Denham, that limping old bard, / Whose fame on *The Sophy* and 'Cooper's Hill' stands; / ... But Apollo advised him to write something more, / To clear a suspicion which possessed the Court, / That 'Cooper's Hill', so much bragged on before, / Was writ by a vicar, who had forty pound for 't."

p. 59, *Wesley*: Sam Westley, with contempt (MS Pate). Samuel Wesley (*c.*1662–1735), Church of England clergyman and poet, father of John and Charles Wesley. He is now considered, as in Swift's day, a minor poet.

p. 59, *Fontenelle*: The French poet, philosopher and scientific writer Bernard le Bovier de Fontenelle (1657–1757).

p. 60, *the lady in a lobster*: Part of the stomach of a lobster (colloquial term used by fishermen).

p. 61, *Dryden, in a long harangue... related*: A scathing reference to Dryden's 'Dedication' to his edition of the *Aeneid*, and in particular his assertion that "Virgil in Latin, and Spenser in English, have been my masters".

p. 61, *his was of gold... iron*: See *Iliad* vi, 234–36.

p. 62, *Alter hiatus in MS*: "Another lacuna in the MS" (Latin).

p. 62, *Blackmore*: The physician and poet Sir Richard Blackmore (1654–1729). His *Prince Arthur: An Heroic Poem in Ten Books* (1695) was modelled on the *Aeneid* and was severely criticized for its slavish imitation of Virgil. Following its publication, Dryden accused Blackmore of plagiarizing his own planned Arthurian project.

p. 62, *Aesculapius*: The Greek god of medicine; a reference to Blackmore's main occupation as physician.

p. 63, *Pauca desunt*: "A few lines are missing" (Latin).

p. 63, *Creech*: Thomas Creech (1659–1700) translator and classical scholar. His translation of Lucretius (1682) won praise from Aphra Behn and John Evelyn, among others. Swift, however, alludes only to his translation of Horace (1684, dedicated to Dryden), which was less than successful.

p. 63, *Ogilby*: The publisher and geographer John Ogilby (1600–76); his translations of Homer, Virgil and Aesop were notable chiefly for the high quality of the printing and paper.

p. 63, *Oldham*: The poet John Oldham (1653–83). The reference here is to his Pindarics.

p. 64, *Aphra the Amazon, light of foot*: The poet and playwright Aphra Behn (*c.*1640–89), another writer of Pindarics.

p. 64, *Never advancing in a direct line*: Pindar is seen to proceed in the same manner as his eponymous odes.

p. 64, *Pindar darted a javelin... degenerate days*: See *Iliad* v, 302–4. See also the *Dunciad* II, 40.

p. 65, *Venus*: An allusion to Cowley's collected love poems, published under the title *The Mistress* in 1647.

p. 66, *your carcass shall... field*: See *Iliad* XXII, 335.

p. 66, *This Venus... her chariot*: I do not approve the author's judgement in this, for I think Cowley's Pindaricks are much preferable to his Mistress. (Note to fifth edition.)

p. 66, *Hiatus valde deflendus in MS*: "A gap in the MS greatly to be deplored" (Latin).

p. 67, *a thousand incoherent pieces*: Bentley was sometimes criticized for his fragmentary knowledge of the Greek poets.

p. 67, *an Etesian wind*: Bentley against Boyle (MS Pate).

p. 68, *In his right hand... in his left*: The person here spoken of is famous for letting fly at everybody without distinction, and using mean and foul scurrilities. (Note to the fifth edition.)

p. 69, *whenever provoked... against his leaders*: See *Iliad* II, 212–64.

p. 69, *Vid. Homer de Thersite*: "See Homer's Thersites" (Latin).

p. 69, *He humbly gave... field*: Bentley had a reputation for using "low and mean" language when aggrieved.

p. 70, *Scaliger*: Most likely a reference to Joseph Justus Scaliger (1540–1609). Known for his acerbic style of argument, Scaliger was criticized by Boyle in his *Examination* and defended by Bentley in his 'Dissertation'.

p. 70, *humanity*: Humanities, i.e. classical literature.

p. 71, *Aldrovandus's tomb*: The Italian naturalist Ulisse Aldrovandi (1522–1605), author of several hundred books and essays cataloguing the results of his botanical expeditions; this oeuvre is presumably his "tomb".

p. 74, *he had got him roaring in his bull*: It is said that Phalaris, tyrant of Acragas *c.*570–554 BC, imprisoned his victims in his brazen bull and roasted them alive. Boyle's translation of Phalaris's *Epistles* depicted a version of this scene in the frontispiece, while his *Examination* concluded: "Many of Phalaris's enemies [...] repented of their vain confidence afterwards in his bull. Dr

Bentley is perhaps by this time, or will suddenly
be satisfied, that he has also presumed a little too
much upon his distance: but 'twill be too late to
repent when he begins to bellow."

p. 74, *For Phalaris was just... faces*: This is according to Homer, who tells the dreams of those who
were killed in their sleep. (Note to fifth edition.)

p. 75, *he drew up nothing... spring*: See Horace,
*Satires* I, 1.

p. 75, *the one he could not distinguish*: Boyle.

p. 76, *Mother*: I.e. the goddess Criticism.

p. 77, *grant me to hit... air*: Wotton's *Reflections*
were published (and had the desired effect of an-
noying Temple), but Temple's reputation was not
harmed, nor was Wotton's substantially enhanced
by the publication.

p. 78, ———: Most probably a reference to Francis Atterbury (1663–1732), bishop of Rochester.
In the early years of his career, Atterbury taught
at Christ Church, Oxford; his students included
Boyle. Atterbury certainly had a hand in Boyle's
edition of the *Epistles*, and it is thought that the
*Examination* published under Boyle's name may

in fact have been the work of Atterbury and fellow Oxford "Ancients".

p. 78, *to take immediate revenge*: The preface to the *Examination* cites Boyle's respect for Temple, "upon whom I so unhappily occasioned this storm of criticism to fall", as one reason for writing.

p. 79, *Philomela's song*: According to Greek legend, Philomela, who was raped by her brother-in-law Tereus, King of Thrace, had her tongue cut out to prevent her telling of the crime. Later accounts held it that Philomela was turned into a nightingale with a beautiful yet melancholy song (see Sir Philip Sidney's 'The Nightingale').

p. 80, *Fain would he... ways*: This is also after the manner of Homer; the woman's getting a painful livelihood by spinning has nothing to do with the similitude, nor would be excusable without such an authority. (Note to fifth edition.)

p. 80, *First, Bentley threw... force*: A reference to Bentley's first 'Dissertation' (1697).

p. 81, *Boyle, observing well... weapon*: Boyle's *Examination*.

p. 82, *Desunt cætera*: "The rest is missing" (Latin).

# Biographical Note

JONATHAN SWIFT was born in Dublin on 30th November 1667, the second and only male child in a family of Anglo-Irish Protestants. His father had died some seven months prior to his birth and, following his mother's return to England, Swift was left from a young age in the care of relatives. In 1673, at the age of six, he began his education at the prestigious Kilkenny Grammar School. In 1682 he entered Trinity College, Dublin, graduating in 1686. The violence surrounding William of Orange's accession to the throne in the "Glorious Revolution" of 1688 brought a temporary halt to Swift's academic career, forcing him to abandon studies for his Master's degree. He found refuge in England, where his mother's connections enabled him to secure a position as an assistant to Sir William Temple. During his residence at Moor Park, Temple's Surrey residence, Swift encountered the then eight-year-old Esther Johnson, later to become the focus of his "Stella" poems and the first in a number of intense but seemingly platonic female friendships that Swift experienced over the course of his life. It was also during this period that Swift first began to display symptoms of Ménière's disease. On the advice of his doctors Swift returned to Ireland in 1690, but returned to Moor Park shortly afterwards. In 1691 he visited Oxford and in 1692 received his MA from Hertford College. In the same year his first poem was published, although Swift's ambitions seem to have remained directed at furthering his career in the Anglican Church. With this in mind he returned to Ireland in 1694 to take on the post of prebendary in the isolated parish of Kilroot, County Antrim. He returned to Moor Park in 1696, where over the next three years he composed both *A Tale of a Tub* and *The Battle of the Books*. Temple's death in 1699 saw Swift return to Ireland again, taking up a clerical position at Laracor. Over the next few years Swift's literary output and his reputation blossomed. He received his Doctorate in Divinity from Trinity College in 1702, and in 1704 *A Tale of a Tub* and *The Battle of the Books* were published in the same volume. This period saw the beginning of his lifelong friendships with fellow writers Pope, Gay and Arbuthnot, and the consequent formation of the Scriblerus Club in 1713. He also began to emerge as a figure in the Whig politics of the day, particularly as an advocate for Ireland. This initiated the production of a number of satirical pamphlets, including the *Drapier's Letters* (1724) and *A Modest Proposal* (1729), and his most famous satirical work, *Gulliver's Travels* (1726). Swift's final visit to England took place in 1727, and following the death of Esther Johnson in 1728 his work became increasingly morbid. His self-written obituary in the form of *Verses on the Death of Dr Swift* was published in 1739 and his health began to decline. He died on 19th October 1745, and was buried in St Patrick's Cathedral, Dublin, next to Esther Johnson.